EASY FORTUNE

A BOUDREAUX SERIES NOVELLA

KRISTEN PROBY

AMPERSAND PUBLISHING, INC.

EASY FORTUNE

A Boudreaux Series Novella

Kristen Proby

Cover Design: Okay Creations

Published by Ampersand Publishing, Inc.

Paperback ISBN: 978-1-63350-092-1

This one is for Indiana Jones, and for all of the fictional journeys he took me on as a child.

CHAPTER 1

~LENA~

*I*t's been a long day. Hell, who am I kidding, it's been a long ass week.

And it's only Wednesday. Thankfully, this is the last week of the school year, and tomorrow is the last day I'll have kids in class. I love being a teacher, and I love my kids, but we're all experiencing burn out by mid-May.

I blow a piece of hair out of my eye and stare at my notes on the dry erase board in my classroom. I teach high school English. I'm giving the final exam for our read-through of The Catcher in the Rye.

It's my favorite book, and I've found that when they participate, the kids like it too. Getting them to do the work is the hard part.

It's hot in here today. Summer in Louisiana isn't for sissies, especially when you work in a sixty-year-old building without air conditioning.

I'm sweating like... well, like I work in an old building without AC.

I wipe the back of my hand over my forehead and glance at my notes when suddenly, the air in the room shifts.

It's subtle, but I feel it. The hair stands up on my neck. I haven't felt this in six years.

"You can get back in your Ferrari and go away," I say casually without looking over at the doorway and do my best to ignore the damn zoo that's come awake in my stomach.

"I don't drive a Ferrari," he replies. His voice hasn't changed at all. It's thick like melted milk chocolate, and he still has his southern accent. I don't know why that surprises me.

"Well, whatever horse you rode in on? Ride back out on it."

I hear him sigh, but I refuse to look at him. Because just one look will suck me in, and I've vowed never to be sucked in by Mason Coulter ever again.

"It's good to see you, Lena."

"Mm hmm." I pretend to study my notes, but I don't actually see the words anymore. "Good to see you, too."

"You haven't even looked over here."

I can hear the smile in his voice. It makes me cringe.

"What do you want?"

"I want you to look at me," he replies.

"Well, we don't always get what we want." Yes, I'm being a bitch, and no, I'm not sorry. Mason was *the one*.

The one that I fell head over heels for, the one that charmed the pants off of me, literally, and then he just left. He disappeared, and I was left here, wondering what in the hell happened. Wondering what I did wrong because I was twenty-two and naïve and so heartsick for him I thought I wouldn't survive it.

But I did.

"So, you're still mad?"

I blink rapidly for a second, and then I can't help it. I turn and take him in, from the top of his gorgeous, dark head to the tip of his designer shoes, and my body immediately comes to life. Panties are singed. And if I thought it was hot in here ten minutes ago, it's an inferno now.

Damn him. He just had to stay hot, didn't he? I mean, couldn't he have lost all of his hair? Gained a whole bunch of weight? *Something*?

"You could say I'm still mad," I reply, proud of myself for sounding calm and indifferent to him, when I'm anything *but* indifferent. "So unless you came in here to tell me you have a terminal illness, you can just turn around and go. I'm not interested in chit chat."

"You were always good at chit chat," he says and flashes that perfect smile at me. But there's something there, in his smile that tells me something isn't quite right.

And I'm just a sucker because I'm about to ask him what it is. I should stay firm and ask him to go.

But first, I need to settle an old score.

"You know," I begin and put the cap on the blue marker. I set it down and turn to fully face him. "The last time I saw you, you said you'd be right back."

"I said I'd see you soon," he says, the smile fully leaving his face now.

"And then you just bailed."

He sighs and leans against the doorjamb. He crosses his arms over his chest and glances down at his shoes, then back up at me. "I owe you an apology for that."

"Yeah. You do."

"I'm sorry." His grey eyes are holding my own, and I can see the sincerity there, hear it in his voice. "I am truly sorry, Lena."

I nod and turn away. "Thanks."

"And I need your help."

Of course he does.

This couldn't be a quick, I want to stop in to see how you are, apologize, and go on my merry way.

No, it has to be complicated.

"My Aunt Claudia passed away last week."

"Oh, Mason." I turn quickly, blinking rapidly. "I'm so sorry. I liked her very much."

He nods. "Thank you."

Mason and his Aunt Claudia were very close. I believe that we all have that one special family member that we bond with, who is important in our lives, and for him, it was his aunt. He spent summers with her here in New Orleans when he was young.

"I hadn't heard that she'd passed." That must be what I see behind his eyes. I don't have the psychic abilities that my best friend, Mallory, has. But I can sense things. I want to hug him, to comfort him, but I stay planted where I am because I know what his touch will do to me.

"I'd planned to come to town and quickly take care of her estate, but it seems Aunt Claudia had other plans." He laughs humorlessly and shakes his head, looking at the ceiling. "The attorney informed me that she was very clear that *you* were to come with me to the reading of the will."

"Me?" I frown. "Why? I only met her a couple of times."

He shrugs and pushes his hand through his hair, in the same way he did six years ago. But now the muscles under his black T-shirt are more defined, tanner from all of the hours he spends outside digging around for old things.

Mason is a well-known and important archeologist.

"You know that she was a bit… *eccentric.*" He smiles. "It's one of the reasons I loved her so much. She did what she wanted, and she wanted this."

"I see." I swallow and stare out of the windows at the trees. There's a slight breeze today. I walk over and open the window, wiggle my fingers and feel the breeze blow in my room. "And if I refuse?"

"If you refuse, her estate will be donated to the city

of New Orleans." My head whips around to stare at him again. "I know, it's a lot of pressure. I don't need her money, Lena. Archeology has been good to me. But I loved her, and I'd like to do right by her."

I take a deep breath and let it out slowly. So, he's not here because he wanted to see me. He's here because his aunt didn't give him a choice. He's right, it *is* a lot of pressure.

"You can think about it," he says. He pulls a business card from his pocket and sets it on the desk closest to him. "That's my cell number. I need to be at the attorney's office on Friday at 2:00 in the afternoon. If you decide you're willing to go with me, I wrote the address on the back."

I nod, staring at the small square of white paper.

"Lena?"

"Yeah?" My gaze finds his again and he smiles, as if remembering something especially sweet.

"You look fantastic. You've hardly changed at all."

"Oh, I've changed."

He nods. "I suppose we both have. He glances up at the white board and my notes. "I loved that book. I read it earlier this year."

I blink quickly, surprised. "For the first time?"

"No, I read it every year." He crosses his arms over his chest and reads the whole board. "I bet I'd pass your test."

"With your eyes closed," I agree with a laugh. "I'm lucky if I can get eighty percent of my kids to read it.

They're not bad kids, they just have other things on their minds, especially this time of year."

"Are Cliffs Notes still a thing?" he wonders.

"Oh yeah," I reply with a nod. "And they're online. There are even apps for that."

"There's an app for everything."

I nod and watch his jaw tick as he takes in my face, my hair. He was always excellent at paying attention. He *saw* me, and that attracted me to him the most of all.

"Think it over," he says and walks toward me. I stand my ground, proud of myself for not backing up. I have no idea what he's planning to do, but I'm suddenly caught up in a strong hug. His arms tighten around my back and he holds me close, rocking me back and forth for a moment.

My God, it's just like I remembered it. How I *dreamed* of for years afterward. Giant butterflies take flight in my belly, goose bumps stand up on my skin. My arms close around his back, and I hug him back. I can feel the remorse, the grief in him, and I can't help but offer him a little comfort. I also can't help but notice how he's transformed in the past six years. He's bulkier, maybe even an inch taller.

Finally, he backs away and smiles down at me. He drags his knuckle down my cheek and I can't stand it anymore. I take a step back, out of his reach. I can't keep a clear head with him touching me. His hand falls to his side.

"I'm sorry. That was probably out of line."

7

"It's okay," I reply. "But I can't promise that I'll be there on Friday."

"I understand." He nods and turns toward the door. "And Lena, if you won't, or can't, come, it's okay. You don't owe me anything."

"No." I nod in agreement. "I don't."

He smiles and turns on his heel and walks out the door. I can hear his footsteps as he walks down the empty hallway and I stay still until I can no longer hear him.

I walk over to retrieve his card and sit in the desk it was sitting on. The writing is simple.

Mason Coulter, Ph.D.

(504) 555-9857

And on the back is the attorney's name and address. Friday at 2:00.

The thing is, I can't even use the excuse that I have school. Tomorrow is the last day of class, and I've already pretty much wrapped things up here. I'll be done by noon on Friday for the summer.

But I do need to think about this. Sleep on it. Talk about it with Mallory and Gram.

Drink some wine.

Tell my body to calm the hell down because we will *not* be going there again, no matter what I decide. Mason was a long time ago, and he made it crystal clear that he didn't want anything from me long ago.

Well, nothing but sex.

And it was pretty spectacular sex at that.

But it messed with me when it was over, and I'm *not* doing that again. No way.

"He's not here for that," I remind myself. He's here because his aunt dictated it, not because he wanted to seek me out.

I need to remember that.

CHAPTER 2

"*A*re you seriously getting rid of these?" Mallory asks me later in the evening. She's sitting on my bed, picking through the clothes and shoes that I've thrown out of the closet.

I'm cleaning it. Cleaning helps me think.

"I never wear them," I reply, looking at the pink flowery sandals she's holding up. "I don't even know why I bought them."

"I'm taking them," she says and sets them in her growing pile.

"You're welcome to anything out there. It's all going to the women's shelter."

"All of it?" she asks in surprise. "Are you becoming a nudist?"

"No." I giggle and sit back on my haunches. I'm rummaging through the shoes on the floor of my small closet. "I really need a bigger place."

"You should just turn your spare bedroom into a closet."

"Yes, but then I wouldn't have a spare bedroom."

"How often do you have visitors?"

I shrug. "Never."

"There you go." She pulls a pink blouse out of the pile and holds it up in front of her, checking herself out in the mirror. Mallory and I have been best friends since we were little. She's a couple of years older than me, but we couldn't be closer if we were sisters. For a lot of years, we only had each other. Aside from our grandmothers, of course. We're different, and kids are always afraid of what they don't understand.

Mallory has psychic gifts, and she is a medium. She's quite powerful, and fought her own talents for many years.

I lean more toward the witch side of things. Spells and magic are my specialty, and I'm the youngest in a long line of witches. My grandmother raised me, and taught me everything she knows.

Well, she *is* teaching me. I don't think I'll ever know everything she does.

"Can I have this pink top?" Mal asks.

"Yes. If it's on the bed, you can have it."

"I think you should bag this all up and set it aside for a few days. You don't want to have remorse later for getting rid of some of this stuff. It's expensive."

"I'm cleaning out the closet," I insist. "I have a ton of crap."

She nods and I sit on my butt and turn to face her, watching as she picks through my yoga pants collection. "How are things with Beau?"

She grins and stares down at her engagement and wedding rings. "Good."

I nod and rest my chin on my knees. "I like him."

"I know. And it's a good thing because he's permanent."

I laugh. "Yeah, about as permanent as you can get."

"So, are you going to tell me what's going on with you?"

"Maybe I just have extra energy because school's almost out and I'm excited about it."

"That's not it."

"You're psychic. You tell me."

"I'm not touching you," she reminds me patiently. "And you only clean and get testy like this when you're upset or have something on your mind."

I wrinkle my nose. "Okay. Do you remember Mason Coulter?"

"The dude you dated right after college? You're the only person I know who would graduate from college and then go *back to college* to take a class that had nothing to do with your major."

I roll my eyes. "It was *interesting*."

"Apparently, because you ended up dating the intern."

"Yeah." I sigh. "He came to my classroom today."

Mal's eyes widen and she tosses another pair of

sandals on her pile, then gives me her full attention. "Seriously? What did he say?"

"His favorite aunt died last week, and he's the only heir. He's in town to settle her estate."

"So, he just dropped in to say hello?"

"No." I shake my head. "No, his aunt, who was a bit eccentric, made a stipulation that he has to take *me* to the reading of the will with him, or else her estate will be donated to the city."

"Of New Orleans?"

"Yes."

"Huh." Mal frowns. "So, were you friends with her after you and Mason stopped seeing each other?"

"No. I only met her a couple of times. She was really nice, and I liked her, but once a guy dumps you, you pretty much sever ties with his family."

"Yeah, that's usually how it works. Interesting."

"So, he came by to tell me that, and of course to ask me to go."

"What did you tell him?"

"That I'd think about it."

Mallory watches me for a moment and then stands up. "I need wine."

"Good call."

I follow her into my kitchen where she finds a bottle of sweet white already open in the fridge. She pours us each a glass and we sit on stools at the breakfast bar.

"Why didn't you tell him yes?" Mal asks.

"You remember how he affected me," I reply and take a long sip of wine. "He just stopped calling me back. I didn't know what I'd done wrong, I couldn't apologize for something. He just...*left*. And it tore me up."

"I know."

"I still have scars from it, and it affects my dating life to this day." Every guy I've dated I've compared to Mason because not one of them made me feel the way he did. Not one of them made me yearn for something more ... something permanent.

"I still say you should go talk to someone," she replies, but I just keep talking.

"Not to mention, even if I didn't still have unre-solved issues, he doesn't deserve to just walk back into my life and ask me to help him."

"It's not really his fault," Mallory says. "It's because of his aunt."

"Stop siding with him."

"I'm not. I'm always on your side. Always. Every time."

"And why does he have to look good? I mean, he's so damn *sexy*."

"Is it me, or did he look like Chris Evans?"

"Don't ruin Captain America for me," I reply. "You know how I love him in those movies."

"Sorry," she says. "But I still stand by my statement. He's a dead ringer for Chris Evans, but he has darker hair. Does he still have dark hair?"

"Yeah. And he's in super good shape. He was in good shape when I knew him years ago, but now? Wowza."

"Did you just say wowza?"

"There's no other word for it. His arms are *ridiculous* with a capital R. Like, they should be illegal in all fifty states."

"Wowza," she says with a sigh. "Beau has good arms too. There's something to be said for good arms."

"And he still hugs good."

"He *hugged* you?"

"Yes. Damn it. He's a good hugger, and his smile is also ridiculous."

"So, everything about him is ridiculous. Sounds like you still have a crush on him."

"I do not." I stand and set my empty wine glass in the sink, and then decide, fuck it. I pour another glass and lean against the counter opposite of Mallory so I can look her in the face. "He may look great, but he was *mean* to me, and I'm not one of those women who just says *it's okay* and sets herself up to be hurt all over again."

"Good because I'd have to slap you if you were." Mal rubs the sweat on the outside of her glass. "Maybe you're overthinking this."

"*Maybe*??"

She laughs and then checks her phone when it beeps with a text.

"Sorry, I'm just going to reply to Beau real quick.

He's asking if I need him to bring anything home for me."

"He's still working?"

"No, he met Eli, Declan, and Ben for dinner." She types out her response and then sets her phone aside. "So, you're totally overthinking this. He hasn't asked you to fuck him. He asked you to go to the reading of his aunt's will, at *her* request. I mean, that's not exactly a date. I haven't been out of the dating pool for long, but I don't think that's *ever* considered a romantic date."

"No," I concede and feel foolish. "You're right. He didn't ask me out on a date. He didn't even suggest that he might be interested in one. He hugged me, but he's grieving and maybe he just needed a hug."

"Exactly. Maybe he just needed a hug, and he knows that you give great hugs. What does he do, anyway? Is he still teaching archeology?"

"No, he got his Ph.D. and he works on dig sites. Not that I've kept track of his career or anything."

I've totally watched his career. But not in a stalkery way. Mal raises an eyebrow and I can't help but bust up laughing.

"Okay, so I might Google his name about once a year, just to see if there's anything interesting to see. But, he doesn't do social media, and there isn't much to read aside from write ups on some of the archeological digs he's been on."

"I would probably do that too." She grins. "So, the

point is, all you have to do is sit next to him in a lawyer's office while the will is read, and then you leave and never see him again."

"Yes."

"It's a no brainer, Lena. You should go. And then you get back to your fabulous life."

"Right." I nod once and pour the last of the wine into my glass. It's only half of a glass, and that's probably for the best. I'm a cheap date. "You're right, and I know I'm going. I'll just have to give myself a pep talk before I go in there. And I'll come to your shop right after to fill you in on it all."

"Well, that goes without saying." She smiles. "What are you doing this summer with all of your time off, anyway?"

"I guess I'll be converting my spare room into a closet. The more I think about that, the more I like the idea."

"You could make it so cool," she says. "I have a whole board on Pinterest dedicated to cool closets. You should check it out. I'll totally help you."

"Okay. That will be fun. I'll look around and find a whole bunch of stuff that I can't afford." I smirk. "But it'll be fun. Not that I have any clothes to put in it anymore. I just gave them all to you."

"I'm telling you, set that stuff aside for a couple of days. Well, except those sandals. I want them."

"You can take them. I'll think about the rest."

She nods. "Are you going to travel this summer?"

"Not really." I tilt my head to the side, considering her. "You rarely ask me what my summer plans are."

"I'm just curious. You should do something fun. You work hard all year long, and you deserve a break. Travel somewhere."

"I don't want to travel alone."

"Take Miss Sophia."

"She's not much of a traveler either. You could go with me."

"I have the shop." She shrugs. "You could come work with me at the shop."

"I don't think it's a good idea for me to take orders from my best friend. I want to actually hang out with you outside of work."

"True. Probably not a great idea."

"What's going on with you? You're antsy."

"You're full of fun words today," she says with a grin. "And there's nothing up. I really just want you to take some adventures. You've always talked about how you'd like to visit places like Paris or Italy. The Boudreauxes have homes almost everywhere. I could hook you up with one."

"I'm not staying at your husband's property," I reply, but then reconsider. "Although, that wouldn't suck."

"No, it wouldn't. And maybe I could come see you for a long weekend or something."

"Are you actually trying to convince me to go live in France or Italy for the entire summer?"

"Why not? You have a free place to stay, and it

would be a great way to recharge your batteries. And maybe I want an excuse to go shopping in Europe."

"You'd hate Europe. Constant dead people talking to you isn't really your thing."

She shrugs. "True, that doesn't sound great, but coming to visit you does. Think about it."

"I will."

Long after Mallory leaves, I'm still thinking about it. Actually, taking some time to myself in a foreign country doesn't sound bad at all.

So that's the plan. I'll go with Mason on Friday to settle his aunt's estate, and then I'll make plans to go spend some time abroad.

This should be easy peasy.

CHAPTER 3

~MASON~

August 22, 1957
My Dearest Love,
I never would have taken this assignment if I'd known how long it would separate me from you. A six-month dig has turned into two long years, and I long for you. I wish you would reconsider joining me, but I understand that you have family obligations in Louisiana.

The ground here keeps uncovering so many treasures. Bodies, perfectly preserved for centuries, fabrics, pottery, even food still inside the bowls. It's as if time has been frozen here, and it's the most amazing find I've ever been on. The people here are kind, but they're nervous about us digging up this sacred ground, worried that we'll anger the gods and that something horrible will happen. Nothing we tell them eases their minds.

I would love for you to be here so I can show this to you. You'd be so excited. Each day is a new discovery.

Please, Claudia, if circumstances change, please come be with me. It would be the adventure of our lives.

Yours always.

Love,

Charles

There are hundreds of letters, just like this one, in the trunk that sits at the end of my Aunt Claudia's bed. My whole life, I would ask her what was in here, and she would just redirect me, showing me books full of wonderful things that came out of the ground.

Old things, old people, preserved for thousands of years and tell me stories about how she helped dig them up.

I knew from the time I was a small boy that I wanted to be an archeologist for a living. I wanted to find amazing treasures and show them to the world.

Aunt Claudia was one of the first women in this country to lead archeological expeditions, and she loved it. It consumed her for much of her life.

But I had no idea that she was once in love. I wish she'd told me *that* story because now all I can think is, where is Charles now? Why did they never marry?

By the time I knew her, Aunt Claudia was a bit of a recluse. She rarely left her big house in New Orleans. She was wealthy, and had a comfortable life here, and I would spend summers with her while my parents were off in Europe. I could have gone with them.

I always chose Aunt Claudia.

I return the letter to its envelope and close the

trunk. It feels like a betrayal to go through her things, but she's gone, and it's going to have to be done eventually. I have to be back in Chile in three weeks, so the sooner I get started, the better.

My phone rings on the floor next to me.

"Hey."

"Hi," My sister, Amelia, says. "How's it going?"

"It's going," I reply and lean back against the bed. The sun went down hours ago. "What time is it?"

"About eleven your time," she says. "What are you doing?"

"I was going through old letters of Claudia's." I rub my hand over my face and realize that I'm hungry. Dinner came and went a long time ago. "I thought I knew her so well, and I'm learning more the longer I'm here."

"She was amazing," Amelia says. "I feel guilty. I should have come with you."

"No, you shouldn't have." I sigh. "You weren't very close to her, and that's okay."

"No one was close to her. Except you."

"We were kindred spirits."

"That's one way to put it," she replies, laughing. "Will it be quick?"

"No." I sigh again. "It seems Claudia had a plan, even in the event of her death. She didn't want a funeral, but she did want me to go to the reading of the will with someone I knew a long time ago when I was interning at Tulane years ago."

"Was this someone you knew also someone you boned?"

I pull the phone away from my ear and scowl at it. "You're twenty. You're not supposed to know about these things."

"Right." She snorts. "Was she?"

"I dated her," I admit. "Claudia met her a few times, and she liked her."

"What's *her* name?"

"Lena." *Lena.* Her name alone stirs something in me, feelings I've spent the past six years pushing to the side. She's sexy as fuck, just like her name, not that I'll tell my baby sister that.

"Lena what?"

"You're nosy. It doesn't matter. She just has to go with me to the appointment with the attorney on Friday. I have no idea why Claudia wanted it that way, but I'm sure I'll find out then."

"Interesting. Did you love her?"

"You know I loved Aunt Claudia."

"Don't be dumb." I can hear her eyes roll through the phone and it makes me smile. "Lena. Did you love Lena?"

I pause, considering the question. "I was very taken with her. She's beautiful and smart, and I enjoyed her."

"Just like a man to not want to admit that he was in love."

"I think I was beginning to fall in love with her," I

reply. "But it didn't work out, and that's for the best. Now, stop asking me nosy questions."

"Never. I'm your baby sister. That's what I do."

I grin, suddenly missing her. "Come to Chile with me next month. I'll put you to work."

"Ugh. No. It's hot there, and there are bugs. You crawl around in the *dirt* for a living."

"You used to like it."

"I just wanted to be where you were. I'll think about it."

I grin and decide to go find something to eat. "Do that. I'll call you after this is all wrapped up."

"Okay. Love you."

"Love you more." I hang up and walk out of Aunt Claudia's room and downstairs to the kitchen. Everything in this old house needs to be updated. I don't think it's been done once in the forty years she lived here.

And, of course, there are no groceries here. It's too late to have something delivered.

Fuck it.

I go out on the front porch and sit on the swing, listening to the night birds. I always loved New Orleans. I should visit more often.

Lena's here.

I frown and watch lightning bugs fly about among the heavy branches of the old oak trees. I still think of Lena often, and wonder how she is. I visited Aunt

Claudia plenty of times over the years, but never looked her up.

I knew I wouldn't be welcome, not after the way I ended it.

I wonder if she'll show up on Friday. I hope so. I don't need Aunt Claudia's money or her estate, but I do want it all to be resolved properly. And it seems Lena is the key to that.

"THANKS FOR COMING, DR. COULTER," Alan Tucker, my aunt's attorney, says as he meets me in the lobby of his firm. He shakes my hand and leads me to his office, and I'm stunned to see that Lena's already sitting there. "You know Ms. Turner."

"Of course." I sit next to her and lean over to whisper, "Thank you."

She smiles and shrugs one shoulder before Alan begins to talk.

"Thank you both for coming in today," he says. "You aunt was very specific about how she wanted this to go, and I'm honoring her wishes."

"As it should be," I reply with a nod.

"Okay, let's get started then." He shuffles some papers aside and pulls a stapled document out of a file folder. "It's actually quite straightforward. I'll read it aloud, and when I've finished, ask any questions you might have."

"Understood."

"*I, Claudia Coulter, declare this as my last will and testament. I revoke all prior wills, and on this 17th Day of June in 2016 declare that I have no spouse and no children. I will all of my real estate, life insurance, monies, jewelry, investment accounts, and any other real property to my nephew, Dr. Mason Coulter.*"

Alan looks up at me with a small smile, and I shift in my chair uncomfortably. I'm sure some people in this position would be excited about becoming an instant millionaire several times over, but I already have wealth.

He clears his throat and keeps reading.

"*There is one condition to this inheritance. Mason and Ms. Lena Turner must immediately embark on a journey, following clues that I've left in places of archeological interest in North America. They must travel together, and must complete the journey together. If they fail to do this, my estate in its entirety will be donated to the City of New Orleans.*"

Lena's head whips over to stare at me, her jaw dropped in surprise.

"Why me?" she asks.

"Ms. Coulter said that would all be revealed during the journey. She also asked me to give you this letter, but you're not to read it until later, when you're alone."

He passes Lena a sealed envelope and crosses his hands over the document on his desk.

"So, we have to go on a scavenger hunt?" Lena demands.

"A treasure hunt," I say quietly, not exactly surprised by this turn of events. "She wants me to hunt for her treasure."

Alan smiles softly. "She does."

"Why do I have to go with him?" Lena asks. Her fingers are shaking. She's upset. I take her hand in mine and give it a squeeze.

"I believe that letter will explain it," Alan replies. "You're due to leave in the morning. The whole trip is already paid for; all you have to do is show up and follow the clues."

"I have to travel with Indiana Jones here, all over North America, hunting for his late aunt's fortune?" She's laughing now, her hand over her face. "This doesn't happen in real life."

"It seems it does," I reply and smile at her when she looks up at me again. Her blue eyes are full of tears from laughter. "But you can choose not to go."

She takes a deep breath and lets it out slowly. "How long will this take?"

"About a week," Alan replies. "You may be able to do it faster, but I suggest you have fun with it. Take your time. Not many people get to go on an adventure like this one."

"Do you already know the details?" I ask him, and he nods happily.

"Your aunt was special, Dr. Coulter."

"I know." My stomach is in knots, my chest tight. I'm so fucking excited to go on this adventure I can hardly stay in my chair. I want to leap up and go *right now*.

But Lena hasn't agreed to go with me, and she's the key.

"School's finished," she murmurs. "Do you need to know right now?"

"I'm afraid so," Alan replies. "Once you agree and leave my office, I set everything into motion. I'll call you both at six in the morning to tell you where to go."

"Six *in the morning*?" Lena demands. "Why would anyone be awake that early?"

I laugh and sit back, watching all of the emotions roll over her face. God, she's fucking gorgeous. Spending the next week, on the ultimate treasure hunt, is going to be spectacular.

She worries her lip between her teeth, thinking it over.

"Can I send a quick text?"

"Of course," Alan says, and we both sit quietly as she types furiously on her phone. A reply comes almost immediately. "Okay. I'll do it."

"Who did you text?" I ask, curious.

"Mallory. She's going to check my mail." She smiles widely. "I might regret this, but I'm in. I might just learn something."

"Are you sure?" I ask and take her hand in mine

again. "I know it's asking a lot, and if you're uncomfortable with it, I understand."

"I'm okay," she says with a nod. "I mean, we'll have separate sleeping arrangements, and—"

"Actually," Alan interrupts, "You'll be sleeping in the same hotel room. Claudia was specific about that as well. She didn't want Mason sneaking out to go find anything on his own. She wanted you to do this *together*. One hundred percent."

"I'm *not* sleeping with him," she says, and I tilt my head to the side. Is that a challenge? Because right now all I can think about is getting her on a plane and joining the mile high club.

"I don't believe she was insisting on the trip to be consummated," Alan says with a wink. "Just that you sleep in the same room."

Lena frowns and sits back in her seat. "Do I have to go to the bathroom and shower with him too?"

Yes to the shower.

"No, ma'am."

She nods. "Okay. Let's do it." She looks over at me and a slow smile spreads over her face. "With Indiana Jones leading the way, we can't lose."

CHAPTER 4

~LENA~

I'm on a freaking plane with Mason Coulter. A *private* plane, headed God knows where, and I'm not freaking out, which surprises me.

Yesterday, when I agreed to do this, I talked myself into seeing this as a great adventure. One I wouldn't get to experience otherwise. I also foolishly believed that I could be alone with Mason and not want to climb him like a tree.

That last part isn't true. Not at all. Because the man is sitting across from me, reading his iPad, sipping coffee. He's in blue jeans and a simple, white button down shirt, untucked. The sleeves are rolled on his forearms, showing off his tan and the chorded veins that run from his hand to his elbow. His dark hair is a bit too long, but even without a fresh haircut, it's sexy. He shaved this morning. And all I want to do is climb in his lap, push my fingers in his hair, and kiss the hell out of him. My whole body is humming in anticipation and excitement.

And sexual tension.

Mason is a toucher. He always was. He puts his hand on the small of my back to lead me to a seat. He covers my hand with his when we're laughing.

He touches me *all the damn time.*

And I like it. A lot. Probably more than I should. I sneak another glance his way and am mortified to find him watching me.

"What?"

"You're thinking awfully hard over there."

"Well, I've been given a lot to think about over the last twenty-four hours."

He nods. "What did the letter say that Alan gave you?"

I smile and cross my legs. "It's a private letter."

He smirks. "Okay. I can respect that."

"Do you know where we're going?"

He shakes his head. "No idea. But I'm excited to get there."

"I can see that. You're like a kid on Christmas morning."

"It's Christmas and my birthday, all rolled into one." He sets his iPad aside and turns to face me. "When I was a young boy, I went on adventures with Aunt Claudia at least once a year. But once I reached about fourteen, she went less and less, until ultimately she was a recluse, staying home."

"That must have been hard for her."

"I agree, but she never complained. I think she just got older, and it was more difficult physically for her to travel."

I nod and sip my water. "It sounds like you're a lot like her."

"I am." He nods and smiles widely, which does *not* help the whole want to climb him like a tree thing. "I sent her photos and stories from my digs often, and she was proud of me."

"Of course she was." The plane dips. "Feels like we're descending."

He looks out the window and points. "Look. I think that's Mount Hood."

"Isn't that in Washington?"

"Oregon," he replies and smiles over at me. "Looks like we're going to Oregon."

"I've never been," I say, suddenly excited again. "What could we possibly be looking for in Oregon?"

"A million different things," he murmurs, still looking outside. The pilot comes over the speakers, telling us that we're about to land in Portland. Mason grins. "Are you ready for this?"

"Yes." I nod. "I'm ready."

We've landed in Portland within a half hour, and as we leave the plane, the pilot passes an envelope to Mason.

There's a rental car waiting for us. Once our

luggage is loaded, and we're in the car, he opens the envelope and I lean over to read it over his shoulder.

Your journey is just beginning. You must be starving. A little Seduction should satisfy you.

We frown at each other. "That sounds like a strip club."

"Portland does have the most strip clubs per capita in the United States," he replies, making me frown deeper. "But I doubt that's it."

"I hope not. It's too early in the day for strip clubs. And I do *not* want to know how you know that little bit of trivia."

He laughs and I pull my phone out of my handbag, typing *Seduction* and *Portland* into Google.

"There's a restaurant here called Seduction."

"That's where we're going," he says. I pull the restaurant up on the GPS and it only takes us about thirty minutes to arrive there. We left so bloody early this morning that it's still before lunchtime, with the time difference, when we arrive.

"They're closed." I point to the hours of operation on the door. "We're too early."

Suddenly, a woman appears and opens the door for us. "Are you Mason and Lena?"

"We are," Mason replies.

"Great, come on in." She opens the door wide for us to step inside, then locks it again behind us. "I'm Riley, one of the owners here. I'm to give you this envelope, and feed you before you go on your way." She leads us to a table, already set with steaming plates of delicious smelling foods.

"You knew we were coming," I say and Riley nods happily.

"Oh yes. This is fun. You must be excited." Mason nods and thanks her for the meal. I had no idea I was so hungry until I dig into the food and sigh in contentment.

"So good."

"Mm," he says. When his plate is half clean, he opens the envelope, reads the clue and then passes it to me.

There's a fire in you that can't be extinguished, not even with all of the water in the lake. You will see.

I blink rapidly and hand it back to Mason. "What lake?"

He's chewing, his brow furrowed, thinking. "I'm not sure. Crater Lake is very popular in Oregon, but I can't think of anything with *fire* there."

"Hmm. Fire. You will see." I nibble on my lip and stare at my water glass.

"What are you thinking?"

"Well, this probably isn't it at all, but the first thing I think of is a fire opal."

"You get an opal out of that clue?"

"I told you it probably isn't right. But fire opals are known to improve sight. They're quite powerful. They also protect against disease and ease pain from grief."

My eyes fly up to his.

"Ease grief," he murmurs and takes his phone out of

his pocket. "You're good, Lena. There is a fire opal mine here in Oregon." He smiles at me. "In Lakeview, to be exact."

I gasp, and then clap my hands. "That has to be it!"

"I agree." He punches more information into his phone and frowns. "It's a six hour drive from here."

I check the time. "That would put us there mid-afternoon. Would that give us enough time to find an opal?"

"It looks like the mine is open until six today, so we should have plenty of time."

"Let's go." We finish our meal, and when Mason tries to pay, Riley just smiles.

"It's all taken care of," she assures him. "Have an amazing journey."

There's a bit of traffic out of Portland, but once on the freeway it opens up, and I sit back, content to watch the scenery as Mason drives.

"It's so green here," I murmur.

"It's a beautiful state," he agrees. He glances my way and then returns his attention to the road. "Tell me about yourself."

I frown. "You know me."

"I *knew* you," he says. "But it's been a while, and people change. Do you enjoy teaching?"

"Very much." Talking about my job is easy. "The kids are fun. Sometimes you get a difficult one, or three, but on the whole, kids just want to be heard. They want kindness, with a little badass thrown in."

"I would imagine that you have the kind badass gig down pat."

"Oh yeah," I reply with a laugh. "Teaching is what I was put here to do. I love it."

"Are you still practicing magic with your grandmother?"

I bite my lip, wondering how to answer this question. One of the things I loved most about Mason when I met him years ago was that he *listened* to me. When I told him about my gifts he didn't recoil and mock me. He asked intelligent questions and didn't judge me.

I'd never met anyone like that in my life, and talking about the craft with anyone that doesn't practice makes me nervous.

"Hey," he says and reaches over to take my hand. "You can still talk to me."

I pull my hand out from under his and shift in my seat. "I do still practice."

"You'd never show me."

"Unless there's a need, it's not something to just randomly show off." I shrug. "Now it's your turn. Tell me about where you've traveled."

"First, we should clear the air."

"Okay." I turn to face him now, pulling one leg under me in the seat. "Where the fuck did you go, Mason? And why did you ignore me? If you didn't want to see me anymore, all you had to do was say so. I'm a pretty reasonable girl."

"I know." He changes lanes and takes an exit, then parks in the parking lot of a McDonald's.

"I'm not hungry."

"I can't drive and concentrate on this at the same time," he says as he turns to face me. "I told you before that I was sorry, and I meant it, Lena. But I'm saying it again. I apologize for the way I handled it, and the way it had to make you feel."

I tilt my head to the side and listen.

"I was young, relatively inexperienced with women because I had focused on academia for so long, and I panicked."

"You *panicked*? It's not like I told you I was pregnant."

"Oh my God, were you—?"

"No. God, no. I'm just saying, there was no reason for you to panic."

"I was offered a job in Tibet. *Tibet*, Lena. And I knew that I had to go. It was everything I'd ever worked for in my life."

"Okay."

"But I didn't want to. I wanted to stay in New Orleans, with you. You'd told me how close you were to your grandmother, and that being in New Orleans was all you ever wanted. I didn't want that life. And we hadn't been together for long. Asking you to go with me—"

"I would have said no."

He nods. "But then I would have been tempted to

stay. I was so fucking lost in you. You're so beautiful, and you were smart and interesting, and everything in my life shifted because of you. I was losing focus on everything I'd worked so hard for."

I blink rapidly, soaking in his words.

"And I knew, I had to just go. I'd worked my *entire* life for that opportunity, and it was the springboard to the rest of my career. I couldn't pass it up."

"No. You couldn't."

"But I hurt you, and I'm so damn sorry, Lena."

"You did hurt me." I nod and look out the wind-shield, blindly watching a traffic signal turn red. "I've worked through some baggage because of that experi-ence. I had trusted you with a lot of myself, emotion-ally and physically. And then you left, without a word, as if I meant nothing to you."

"I wish I could undo it. Or at least have this conver-sation six years ago."

"You could have been honest with me," I reply and turn to face him, much of the old animosity gone. Because the truth of it is, he *was* young, and so was I. "You can always be honest with me. It would have still hurt, but I wouldn't have wondered what I did wrong to make you go."

"You didn't do anything wrong." He leans over and cups my cheek. "The only thing you did was be every-thing wonderful and sweet. And I'm sorry that I ever made you doubt that. Can you forgive me?"

I swallow hard, unable to look away from him. "Just

don't do it again. I know this time is different, and that I'm here because of your aunt, but when you leave, just tell me you're leaving."

"I can absolutely promise that I won't ever just disappear on you ever again."

"Okay." I nod and take a deep breath. "I don't know about you, but I feel better now."

"Me too."

"We'd better go, or we'll get there too late."

"We could go in the morning."

"We might have to travel again all day tomorrow."

"Good point." He pulls back onto the freeway and takes my hand in his, then kisses my knuckles. "Thank you."

"Just drive, Dr. Jones."

"I love Indiana Jones," he says with a smile.

"Me too."

"WE'RE CLOSING IN A HALF HOUR," the man behind the counter says. We've just arrived, both of us panting from running in from the parking lot. "What's your name again?"

"Mason Coulter."

"I'm Ted." He smiles and reaches out to shake Mason's hand. "And you must be Lena."

"I am."

"You actually have excellent timing," Ted says and

locks the door, turning the sign to closed. "The last group of tourists just left a few minutes ago, and for what I have to show you, well, you'll see."

He winks and motions for us to follow him out back. The weather is beautiful today, and the hottest part of the day is over, leaving us with a pleasant evening.

"What are these buckets?" I ask Ted.

"These are the buckets we give to customers to sift through, looking for opals," he replies. "We do the actual mining, and customers pay for the bucket, then sift through them."

"That seems like cheating," I reply, earning a smile from Mason.

"It's easy," Ted says with a shrug. "And profitable for us. Not to mention, you wouldn't imagine the liability cost of allowing people down into the mine."

"Oh, that makes sense," I reply with a nod. "So where are we going?"

"Into the mine," Ted says with a smile. "Something tells me that Mason wouldn't be content with a bucket."

"You'd be right," Mason replies with a laugh. "But your operation here is impressive, and for novice customers, it's perfect."

"Thank you," Ted says as he passes us each helmets. "We're not going in deep, but you never know what might fall. We're going to dig for a bit, and then you can sift through what we pull out."

"Fun," I reply and watch in awe as Ted sets about pulling dirt from the ground. The operation is bigger and louder and just *more* than I ever expected.

Before long, we're standing before a huge, square machine that sifts the earth, making the dirt and sand fall through the mesh and leaving behind large rocks.

"We've got it from here," Mason says to Ted when we have plenty of earth to wade through. "Do you need us to leave soon?"

"Take your time," he says with a wink. "I'll be where you found me."

Ted walks away and Mason begins to show me how to find our opals. "Like this," he says, shaking the box. The dirt falls away, and there's nothing left.

"Well, that was a dud," I say as Mason shovels more in.

For the next half hour it's the same. We shimmy and shake the box, and we're left with rocks or nothing at all.

Until, finally, we hit the motherlode.

"Look at that," Mason says and holds a rock up.

"It just looks like a pretty rock." He turns it over, and I gasp. "Oh, it's beautiful."

It's brilliantly red and orange.

"Can you imagine how pretty it'll be when it's polished?" Mason asks. "This is a beauty."

"So pretty," I agree and rub my finger over the smooth side. We did it! We found what his aunt wanted us to find.

I can't help it, I launch myself into his arms for a big hug. "I'm so proud of us!"

He laughs and hugs me back, and as I begin to pull away, he kisses my cheek. I still and stare into his eyes, and the next thing I know, he's kissing me. Not a gentle kiss, but a crazy, passionate kiss that I feel all the way down to my toes.

I pull away and blink my eyes open. We're both breathing hard, and I want him more in this moment than I've ever wanted anyone in my life.

So I pull away, pat his shoulder, and say, "Good job."

I march away toward the main building, cursing myself.

Good job??? He kisses me like his life depends on it, and I say good job.

I roll my eyes. Way to go, Lena.

CHAPTER 5

~MASON~

*S*he's so much more than I remember. She was always funny, and smart. Sexy. But it's like she's all of that times one hundred.

And I'm quickly learning that I'm pulled to her in that inexplicable way all over again.

She's marching ahead of me at a fast clip after her *good job* remark, which I can't help but laugh at. The kiss was unexpected, and her reaction is encouraging.

She wants me as well.

It will be interesting to see how long we can keep our hands off of each other while on this trip.

Without looking back at me, she storms into the main building, letting the door slam behind her. I follow her in, the stone heavy in my pocket.

"How did you do?" Ted asks.

"Fantastic," I reply and show him our opal.

"That's a beauty," he says with a nod. "Good job."

Lena chokes, coughs, her face turning bright red.

"Are you okay?" Ted asks, but she just nods, and I can't help but laugh again.

"Inside joke," I inform him. "What do I owe you for this?"

"Nothing," he replies and reaches under the counter. He passes me two white envelopes this time. "The top one is the name of your hotel, the room number, and your keys. The other is your next clue."

"Wow, every detail has been taken care of," Lena says in surprise as we walk out to the car.

"Doesn't surprise me." I open the hotel information first, and pull it up on my GPS. "The hotel is close by."

"Thank goodness," she says with a sigh. "I'm ready for food and a shower."

I nod, not wanting to think too hard about a wet, naked Lena while I'm in the same room with her. My dick is already permanently semi-hard just from being so close to her.

"Let's find our room, get some food, and then we'll open the clue."

"Sounds good," she says with a nod. "And about the *good job* comment—"

"Don't." I shake my head and smile at her. "It's maybe one of my favorite moments with you. You're a fun delight, Lena."

"A fun delight," she says with a laugh. "I've been called worse."

The hotel is close by, and our room is a simple, double bed room on the second floor.

"Nothing fancy," I say as we wheel our bags inside.

"It's a tiny town," she replies. "I'm happy if it's clean."

And it is. The bathroom is small but clean and functional, and we'll only be here overnight anyway.

"Food," she insists. "I saw a Denny's about a block away."

"I'm fine with that if you are."

"So fine with it," she replies with a nod, already walking to the door. "Feed me, Dr. Jones."

"Are you going to call me that all the time?"

"Yes." She laughs.

"Miss Jade is a tricky one. *You might get wet.*" Lena reads the clue aloud again and then stares off into space. She's sitting on her bed, cross-legged. She's in yoga pants and a simple T-shirt, her blonde hair is piled on top of her head, and I want nothing more than to strip her naked and explore every fucking inch of her.

This whole two bed thing is out of the question going forward.

"Jade is my middle name," Lena informs me. "I'm told it's because jade inspires peace and calm."

"Do you feel calm and peaceful?" I ask, stretching out on my bed, my hands tucked behind my head.

"Not usually," she says with a smile. "I admit, I'm lost on this one."

"I'm not."

Her gaze whips up to mine in surprise. "What? Why didn't you say something?"

"Because you're beautiful when you're thinking hard."

She scoffs, but her cheeks turn the prettiest shade of red. I want to watch them flush for other reasons entirely.

"I'm quite sure she wants us to go hunt for some jade at Big Sur, California."

"Oh, fun!" She claps her hands and immediately reaches for her phone, presumably to search Google. "I had no idea that you could find jade there. I've always wanted to see Big Sur. The photos I've seen are amazing."

"It's beautiful," I agree. "Or I'm told."

"You haven't been either?"

I shake my head no.

"Good. We will see it together." She smiles as she pages through her phone, and then frowns. "It's another nine hour drive tomorrow."

"So we'd better leave early."

She nods and plugs her phone in, then climbs under the covers.

"Good night."

She falls asleep quickly, but I'm awake for a long while after her. I know she's not indifferent to me. When I came out from the shower her eyes traveled over my body like she was memorizing every inch of me. Of course, I wasn't naked, but I want to be. I don't know if we could have a relationship, but I want her.

And I'm going to have her.

"I HOPE this whole trip isn't a road trip," Lena says the next day as we pull into Big Sur. "Nine hours is a long time."

"I agree." We left later than I'd hoped because we both slept in, and by the time we ate and got on the road it was close to nine in the morning.

But we're not on a schedule.

"Do we know where we're staying?" she asks.

"Yes, when I checked out of the hotel this morning, the lady asked me if we'd figured out the clue. When I told her we're headed to Big Sur, she handed me an envelope with hotel information."

"I'm seriously impressed with how well executed this whole thing has been. And we're only on the second clue."

"I admit, I'm impressed as well." I pull into our hotel and we both go inside to check in.

"Oh yes, Dr. Coulter. Your room is ready." The front desk woman passes me two keys. "And you're in luck.

Low tide is in about thirty minutes. So go drop your things off in your room, and then head on out."

"Are we going to need tools for this?" Lena asks.

"Yes. I have a flashlight and a bag here for you," she replies and passes it to me.

"The beach is rockier than I expected," Lena says when we make it down there a little later. "I was expecting sandy beaches."

"Those are farther south," I reply with a smile and hold her hand while she gingerly chooses her footing down to the shore. "This is more rugged."

"It's gorgeous," she says. "Are there sharks here?"

"Probably."

"Not going in the water," she says, shaking her head adamantly. "Where do we find the jade?"

"From what I understand, we just look around the tide pools. They might be under other rocks."

She nods and immediately gets to work, picking through rocks. "I found a starfish."

"Those live in the ocean too."

She sticks her tongue out at me, and continues to look around.

"Look!" She holds up a rock with a green tint. "Is this it?"

"That's it," I reply. "It can be red, too."

"I know." She slides the rock in her bag and continues to work. Over the next hour we explore, finding several good sized pieces of jade, and enjoying the time together.

"It smells good here."

I stop to take a deep breath. "Nothing like it."

"Look at these smooth rocks." She's walking away from me, over smooth rocks that the tide has worn down over many years.

"Be careful, they're slick."

"I'm fine." But suddenly her arms flail about and she loses her balance, falling into the water.

The tide is beginning to come back in, so it's about waist deep where she is. I wade out to help her up and back to shore. She's sputtering, pushing her hair off of her face.

She's soaked.

"Damn it," she mutters.

"I didn't warn you soon enough."

"Did I lose my rocks?"

"No." I laugh and take the bag from her, and watch as she wrings her hair out. "It's safe."

"Good." She sighs. "I'm cold and I need a shower."

"Indeed." I reach my hand out for her and she takes it, holding on tight as I lead her back to the hotel. The sun is just beginning to set.

When we reach our room, I put our treasure aside, and immediately walk into the bathroom and start the shower.

"I don't want you to get sick. We need to warm you up."

"I'm not stripping down in front of you."

49

My lips twitch as I watch her prop her hands on her hips and look at me defiantly.

"No, ma'am. I wasn't suggesting such a thing." But I cross to her and kiss her forehead. "But, if you wanted to do that, I wouldn't complain."

I wink and walk away, leaving her to shower and get comfortable. In the meantime, I call down for room service. Steaks, salads, and cheesecake for dessert sounds good.

She's not out yet when the food arrives, so I wheel the tray to the far side of the room where we can watch the sun sink down behind the water.

"You didn't have to do that."

I turn at the sound of her voice and feel my breath catch. Without any direction, or realizing that I'm doing it, I stand and walk to her. She's wrapped in a towel, her hair washed and still damp.

"I tried to dry my hair, but hotel blow dryers suck."

I push my fingers through the strands. "You are so beautiful, Lena."

She swallows hard, watching me.

"I'm sorry that I didn't take my clothes in the bathroom with me. I didn't think about it."

She's slowly leaning toward me, as if she can't help it.

Her hands are fisted in my shirt at my sides, her eyes staring at my throat.

"Lena?"

"Yes."

She doesn't look up.

"I want you."

She swallows hard again and then finally meets my eyes with hers.

"I want you, too."

That's all I need. My lips are on hers, my hands buried in her damp hair as I feast on her. She reaches up to grip onto my shoulders and her towel simply falls, pooling at her feet.

I step back to look at her. She moves to cover her breasts, but I stop her.

"No. Don't cover yourself." She bites her lip. "God, Lena, you're stunning."

"You've seen it before."

"I was a fool." I reach out and touch her already tight nipple with the back of my finger. "I should have cherished you more."

"You were gentle with me."

"That's not the same thing." My eyes find hers again and I lift her in my arms, then lay her gently on the bed. "I want to explore every inch of you."

"Well, you *are* an explorer," she says with a grin. "But you're terribly overdressed."

"Would it make you feel better if I were naked too?"

She smiles and nods. How can I resist her?

I step back from the bed and shrug out of my shirt, my pants, and underwear and stand before her in just what God gave me.

"Wow."

"You've seen it before," I say, echoing her words.

"You've changed," she murmurs. "You were hand-some before, but damn, Mason."

I grab her small foot and kiss it as I kneel on the bed. I kiss up to her knee, making her fall back against the pillows.

"You're serious about this," she says.

"Never been more serious about anything in my life."

"Do I get to return the favor?"

"Later."

She gasps when my tongue slides up her inner thigh. Her skin is soft and still dewy from the shower.

I glide my nose along the crease of her leg and her hands fist in the blankets.

She's so damn responsive.

"You smell like you want me inside you."

"Because I do," she murmurs.

"Soon." I lick the outer lips of her pussy and grin when she moans. "First, I get to learn you all over again."

"You're going to kill me."

"But what a way to go."

I smile up at her before I plant my tongue on her clit, then slide down into her lips and kiss her inti-mately. She's writhing, her legs moving in agitation.

"Mason."

"Mm hmm."

She fists my hair in her hands and holds me to her,

her hips moving against my mouth until she comes beautifully. Her whole body flushes, and she moans until her whole body just lets go.

"Now." I climb over her and poise my cock against her pussy. "I need to be inside you right now."

"Yes."

"I don't have any condoms." I stare down at her, so pissed at myself for not bringing any.

"I have the birth control covered," she says with a grin. "And I'm healthy."

"Do you want to see my medical records?" I ask, making her laugh.

"No, I want you to fuck me."

I push just the tip inside and lean my forehead against hers. "I'm not going to fuck you."

"No?"

"No." I push farther and stop. "I'm going to make you crazy."

"Good."

I push all the way in now and grind my pubis against her clit.

"I'm going to make you scream."

"Thank God."

My hips begin to move; I couldn't stop them if I wanted to. "But I'm not going to fuck you."

"Whatever you want to call it."

I grip her hand in mine and pin it to the bed over her head, and reach under her ass with the other hand to angle her up just a bit. I can't stop myself from moving faster, driving us both to the edge of reason.

She's holding on with all her might. I rest my lips against hers.

"Come, baby."

And just like that, her back arches and she comes apart under me. It's the most beautiful thing I've ever seen, and I follow her over the edge, succumbing to my own orgasm.

CHAPTER 6

~LENA~

"This flight is damn bumpy," I say as I grab the armrest for dear life. We're back in the private plane, heading God knows where.

"I'll take a bumpy flight over another ten hour drive," Mason replies. When the plane dips again, and I gasp, he pulls me into his lap and holds me close. "You're okay."

"Shouldn't I have my seatbelt on?"

"I've got you," he replies and kisses my lips softly.

"I think you're trying to distract me," I whisper against his mouth.

"Is it working?"

"Oh yeah." I grin and sigh when he kisses me again. His hand glides up my bare leg and under the skirt I'm wearing. When I packed for the trip, I had no idea we'd be doing so many *outdoorsy* things. Those fingers clench onto my bare ass and I bite his lower lip. "How can you turn me on so much when I'm pretty sure we're going to die?"

"We aren't going to die," he replies. He stands with me still in his arms and then lays me down across the bench seats. He kneels next to me and kisses my cheek, then my neck. His hand slides up between my thighs and he smiles when his fingers reach my pussy. "And you are *very* turned on."

"Have you seen you?" I ask and reach for the zipper of his pants. "Not to mention, you never stop touching me, and your hands are ridiculous."

"Ridiculous?" he asks with a raised brow. "You think doing this is ridiculous?"

He sinks a finger inside me and I'm pretty sure I couldn't tell you my name if you asked.

"We're in an airplane."

"Thank you, sweetheart," he says with a smile. "I didn't realize."

"Smart ass."

"We have a pilot and a co-pilot. No one is back here." He wiggles his eyebrows. "We can do whatever we want."

"We could land at any moment."

"You're overthinking again." He clicks his tongue and shakes his head and slips another finger in to join the first.

"Shit." My back arches. "You're teasing me."

"Just getting you warmed up." His grey eyes are on fire as he watches me closely. His fingers are doing crazy things to me and all I know for sure is, I want him.

Now.

"Mason," I say and then gasp when he presses his thumb to my clit. "Take your pants off."

"Is that an order?"

"Yes."

He cocks a brow.

Accepting the challenge, I push his hand away and plant my hand on his shoulder, urging him down to the floor of the plane. His lips twitch as he watches me take over the control, but after I've unfastened his pants and pulled his already hard cock out of the pants, all humor has fled his face.

He's expecting me to climb on top of him and ride him, but instead I lick the rim of the head of his dick and smile when he sucks air in through his teeth.

"My turn," I murmur and go to work, sucking and licking, touching, pulling. He buries his fingers in my hair and holds on as I work him over. And just when I think he might be getting close to coming, I crawl on top and sink over him, taking him all the way in. I begin to move, but he sits up and plants his hands on my ass, guiding me up and down.

He's so tall that his eyes almost meet mine. Neither of us talks. We're here, in the moment, in this place, making each other crazy.

I can feel the orgasm move through me, and I clench down on him as it washes over me. His hands tighten on my ass and he pushes up, hard, losing himself in me.

The pilot comes over the speakers.

"We'll be landing in about forty minutes."

Mason grins. "Excellent timing."

By the time the wheels touch down, we're both put back together and smiling smugly at each other.

The pilot comes out of the cockpit and passes Mason a letter.

"When you're finished, come back to the plane."

"We're not staying?"

"No."

Mason nods and ushers me down to the tarmac where another rental car is waiting. We climb inside, leaving our luggage aboard the plane, and Mason opens the envelope.

"Well, this I know nothing about."

I grin and hold my hand out. This clue wasn't a letter from Aunt Claudia. It's a card.

A tarot card.

"It's the Thunderbolt card," I murmur. "Frankly, when this card turns up during a reading, it makes most people nervous."

"Why?"

"Because it usually means that there's about to be a significant change in one's life, but not in a good way. It brings great upheaval. The good thing is, it usually means that it's for the best, but it's disruptive none-theless."

"Hmm." His eyes narrow as he studies the card.

"Do we even know where we are?" I ask, realizing that I didn't hear the pilot say.

"No." He pulls his phone out of his pocket and brings up the GPS. "We're in New Mexico."

"Okay. I have no idea what we might find in New Mexico. Aside from really good TexMex food."

His lips twitch in good humor as he thinks. He snaps his fingers. "I know where we're going."

"Great. Where?"

"We're going to find Thunder eggs."

He tries to start the car, but it doesn't turn over.

"Seriously, the rental place gave us a car with a bad battery." He sighs and moves to get out of the car, but I lay my hand on his arm and shake my head.

"I've got this."

He frowns, but watches as I mumble a few words, wiggle my fingers, and the car starts. He raises a brow. "Good job."

I can't help it, I throw my head back and laugh. He's not shocked, or repulsed, or afraid.

He's acting like he sees witches do this every day of his life, and nothing could put me at ease more effectively.

He pulls away from the plane and away from the airport.

"Do you know where we're going?"

"Yes," he says with a smile. "Aunt Claudia brought me here a couple of times."

"Okay, what is a thunder egg, exactly?"

"It's a rock," he says as he changes lanes, "that when you break it open, there is amethyst, or rose quartz, or something equally beautiful inside."

"A geode," I reply with a smile. "They're beautiful. I've never had the chance to find them, though."

"They were a common gift from Claudia. I have dozens. All different shapes and sizes."

"Do they just lay out in the open?"

"Yes." He nods. " You dig for the best ones, but this will be a quick challenge."

We arrive at a parking lot where several cars are already parked.

"I'm not dressed for this."

He looks me up and down, his eyes hot with lust as he does, and just shrugs. "If we have to dig, I'll do the dirty work."

"That's very chivalrous of you," I reply with a laugh. Mason glances in the backseat of the car and grins.

"They gave us a pick." He reaches in and comes out with what looks like a tiny pickaxe. "This will make it easier."

"If you say so. You're the expert."

He reaches for my hand and leads me down a dusty path. There are men with hats on to protect themselves from the sun milling about. They have bags hanging from their waist, and they're scanning the ground.

"This must be lucrative."

"It can be," Mason says with a nod. "The thunder

rocks look jagged, almost shaped like cauliflower on the outside."

"I hate cauliflower." I wrinkle my nose, making him laugh. "But I like pretty, sparkly things."

He veers us off the path to what looks like a mound of dirt.

"Stand back," he says. "It's about to get pretty dusty here."

And with that, he begins to ferociously attack the dirt, picking away at it until a rock falls out of it and down toward me.

It's the size of a soft ball, and definitely looks like what we're looking for.

"I bet this is a good one," I say as Mason joins me. "How do we break it open?"

He takes it from me, lays it on the ground, and smacks it with the pickaxe. It breaks into two pieces, showing off a gorgeous pink center.

"Oh, that's a pretty one."

"Rose quartz," he says, examining it. "This was formed by a volcano."

"We're standing on a volcano?"

"An ancient one," he says with a nod. "This was once lava, probably about a million years ago. All of the pressure over so much time formed this pretty quartz."

"You're pretty smart, Dr. Jones." I take one of the halves from him and study it. "I'm keeping this half."

"Of course." He kisses my cheek and then my neck.

"We should probably head back. Sounds like we have another flight in store for us today."

"Let's take a minute," I reply. "Alan suggested we take our time and enjoy the adventure. There's no reason that we can't walk around and see what we can find."

"It's hot out here."

"I'm not suggesting we stay for hours." I bat my eyelashes at him, making him grin.

"As you wish."

"Now you're quoting my favorite movies."

"What's not to like about the Princess Bride?"

"Exactly." I link my fingers with his and we take a stroll around the desert, looking for rocks. "Are there rattlesnakes out here?"

"Probably." He glances down at me, then back at the ground. "Are you afraid of animals?"

"Why do you ask?"

"Because you asked if there were sharks in the ocean, and now rattlesnakes."

"Well, wildlife isn't something to scoff at," I reply. "You should always be aware of what could kill you."

"That's not a bad motto to live by. You should make it into a bumper sticker."

"I'm serious."

"So am I." He laughs. "What happened in your youth to make you so wildlife-conscious?"

"I was almost eaten by an alligator."

"Really?"

"Really. We were out in the Bayou, at Mallory's grandmother's house, and Mallory and I were running around on the boardwalks that ran between her grandmother's house and my grandmother's house."

"There are a lot of grandmothers and houses in this story."

"Two of each," I agree. "Anyway, we were running and being silly young girls. I was ahead, and I glanced back to see where Mallory was, and my shoe caught in one of the boards. I fell into the swamp water."

"Ew."

"No kidding. It's gross anyway, but unbeknownst to me, there was a giant alligator in the water, and he wasn't super happy with sharing his space with me."

"Jesus, Lena."

"I was petrified. I didn't swim well. Mallory was screaming, and this huge dinosaur was swimming right for me. Gram must have heard Mallory screaming and came running out, plucked me right out of the water, just as the alligator reached me."

"I think I'd be afraid of wildlife after that too."

"I just like to know what might be lurking about."

He pulls me to him and hugs me tightly, rocking me back and forth under the scorching New Mexico sunshine.

"I just found another thing about you that makes me like you even more," he says.

"What, that an alligator almost ate me?"

"Well, I can't fault the alligator. You're delicious." He

bites my neck, sending shivers through me. "No, you just used unbeknownst in a sentence."

"Unbeknownst is a great word," I reply. "It's fun to say. It might be my *favorite* word. What words do you like?"

"Whilst," he says. "That whole *st* sound at the end of a word is pleasant, isn't it?"

I nod. "I also like soliloquy."

"That rolls nicely off the tongue," he says with a nod. "I have a bunch of dirty words that I like as well. But I'll have to tell you those later, when I can point them out to you."

"I always did enjoy show and tell."

"Excellent," he replies. "We're going to have a fun session of show and tell tonight then."

"I can't wait."

CHAPTER 7

*I*f I thought the flight earlier today was bumpy, I was mistaken. That was mild compared to the flight we're on now.

"Seriously, are they *aiming* for the rough air?" I ask and hold onto the armrest for dear life.

"This is a smaller plane," Mason replies. "It can't fly as high as commercial flights. So, yeah, we're going to hit more air."

"It's not a good time." I swallow hard and wipe the sweat from my forehead.

"I'm sorry, sweetheart." He kisses my cheek and just takes my hand in his. We're both seated with our belts on, and he's not offering to do me on the floor of the plane, so it's definitely a rough ride.

"We'll be landing soon. Sorry for the bumpy ride, folks," the pilot says over the sound system.

"Ugh." I shut my eyes, but that just makes it worse.

"Have you always had motion sickness?" Mason asks.

"Yeah." I shrug. "It's gotten better as I've gotten older, but I avoid theme parks. Rides aren't fun for me. Do you like the big roller coasters?"

"I haven't spent a lot of time on them," he says, shaking his head. "But I do love things like the Eye in London, or a ferry ride around Seattle."

"Big kid rides," I reply with a smile. We're descending, and the plane isn't bouncing around quite as bad now. "I wonder where we're going now?"

"I think we're headed east."

"How do you know?"

He tucks a lock of my hair behind my ear. "Just a hunch."

Just when I think the plane is leveling off and I might catch a break from the turbulence, it starts again, but worse this time.

The next thirty minutes are the worst of my life. Finally, when we're on the ground, all I can do is breathe in and out through my nose.

"Are you okay?" Mason asks. I quickly shake my head no. "No more hunting today. We'll go to the hotel and regroup."

"It'll be okay."

"No." The tone of his voice makes me turn to look at him. "This isn't a race, Lena. We can take the rest of today to relax and get back at it tomorrow."

"I could use some down time," I admit. Even though

I've done a lot of sitting in planes or cars between the actual events, I'm exhausted. "Traveling is exhausting."

"Absolutely." As soon as the plane stops and the pilot opens the cockpit door, Mason takes my hand and helps me stand. The pilot hands him an envelope and when we deplane, there's another car waiting for us.

"Welcome," an older woman says as we approach the car. "I'm not supposed to tell you much of anything except here is an envelope with your hotel information. Just let the hotel know when you're finished and ready to leave and the plane will be ready for you."

Mason nods, but all I can do is scowl.

More flights.

Yuck.

We get in the car, but before we can read the clue, my phone pings with a text from Mallory.

Are you in North Carolina yet?

I frown and call her, putting her on speaker phone.

"Hey," she says. "Are you and the sexy Captain America in North Carolina?"

I smirk. "I don't know, but the sexy Captain America, aka Indiana Jones, can hear you. You're on speaker."

"Hi, Mason," she says.

"Hello, Mallory."

"I think you look like Chris Evans with darker hair."

"I will take that as a compliment."

"Oh, it is," she insists. "Pretty much every woman in America wants to do Captain America."

Mason laughs, and I slap my hand over my eyes, mortified.

"So are you in North Carolina?"

"I don't know," I reply. "We just landed. How do *you* know where we might be?"

"Uh, psychic, remember?"

"Right." I giggle and Mason checks his phone.

"We're in North Carolina," he confirms. "Charlotte, to be exact."

"Okay, well, you guys have fun."

"Love you," I reply. "Good bye."

"Bye!"

I hang up and sigh loudly. "She's brutally honest."

"Do *you* want to do Captain America?" he asks, his lips twitching with humor.

"I mean, I probably wouldn't turn him down." I shrug. "But I don't think you look like him."

"No?"

"No." I shake my head and decide, what the hell? I don't have anything to lose. "I think you're better looking."

"Now you're just feeding my ego."

"No. You're pretty sexy. You always were."

He kisses the back of my hand. "Thank you."

I open the hotel envelope and am relieved to see on an included map that we don't have far to go to reach our accommodations. "This is nearby."

"Excellent."

Once we're checked in and we arrive at the room,

all I want to do is order room service and pass out. But when we walk inside, I can't help but notice that there's only *one* bed.

"Was this your doing, or a mistake by the hotel?"

"It's no mistake," he replies easily, setting our bags by the closet. "I don't plan to sleep without you again in the near future."

But then you'll leave and I'll be sleeping alone again.

I don't say that; I simply raise a brow. "What if I don't want to sleep with you?"

He narrows his eyes at me. "Would you prefer your own bed?"

"No."

He advances on me, slowly, those grey eyes still narrowed. He looks quite menacing, but I don't move an inch. I raise my chin as he gets closer, maintaining eye contact.

"Are you being sassy?"

"I don't know if you know this about me," I reply, "but I am quite sassy all the time."

"Are you still feeling ill?"

"A little. But now that I'm on the ground, it's not so bad."

"Good. Because I'd like to get you naked and make you moan under me."

"Can we get food too?"

He smiles now. "Yes. Moaning is first."

"Food first," I reply sternly. "I'm hungry. I need the calories."

He shrugs. "I can compromise."

"Good." I nod and turn to walk away, but he catches my arm and spins me back to him, pressing me against him. He cups my cheek and kisses me long and slow, making my whole body hum.

"There is no one else I'd rather be on this adventure with," he says softly. "Thank you for agreeing to come. You're amazing."

"I'm amazingly hungry," I reply and kiss him again. "And you're welcome."

"THE HILLS ARE as green as what you'll find inside them."

Mason reads the clue the next morning and frowns.

"Emeralds," I reply.

"How do you come to that?"

"Well, we've done nothing but chase precious stones, and I'm gonna go out on a limb and say that stones are our theme. Emeralds are green."

"Makes sense," he says with a nod. "I'll bet there's an emerald mine nearby."

Google is my friend, and doesn't disappoint. "There's a place called Emerald Hollow Mine not far from here."

"Let's go," he says. Once in the car, headed down the highway, I slide my sunglasses on and reach over for his hand.

"I wonder how many of these she's going to have us do?"

"No idea," he says. "But I'm having fun with you."

"Me too." I grin and roll my window down to enjoy the sunshine. The air smells fresh. "It's a beautiful day."

Before long, we arrive at the public mine and walk into the small office. We're greeting by a man with kind eyes and permanently dirty skin.

"We've been expecting you," he says with a smile. "Come with me."

We follow him out to a huge field of nothing but dirt. He passes us each a shovel and a bucket. "All you have to do is fill your buckets and then meet me over at that covered area and we'll sift through it. You might get lucky and find some emeralds."

He nods and walks away.

"He's a man of few words," I mutter. "And we get to dig in the dirt. Again."

Mason chuckles and sticks his shovel in the dirt. "A little dirt never hurt anyone."

"No, but you're used to digging around in it. I'm not."

"Do you want me to fill your bucket?"

"No." I follow his lead and scoop dirt into my bucket. "I didn't say I *couldn't* do it."

He nods and waits for me to finish with my bucket and then leads me over to the covered area where several people are sitting, sifting their dirt through contraptions very similar to the one we used at the opal mine.

An hour later, and five emeralds richer, we leave the mine, headed toward the airport with a new clue envelope.

"I'm gonna open it."

"Do it," Mason says.

I scan it and frown. *"Your last clue was your last clue. You'll be flown to your final destination, and all will be revealed to you there."*

"We're almost done," he says and glances my way.

"Time sure flies when you're having fun." My voice is light, but I can't help but feel sad. We have one more adventure, probably just one more night together, and then we'll go our separate ways again. I've known from the beginning that it would end like this, but saying goodbye is going to hurt.

If I didn't know better, I'd say that I was falling in love with Mason Coulter all over again.

But I'm not. I *can't.*

Because he isn't going to stay.

We're quiet as Mason drives us back to the airport and we board the plane. Our bags are taken care of.

"I'm going to miss being pampered like this." I grin and grab a bottle of water on my way to my seat. "A girl doesn't get to fly in a private plane every day."

He smiles softly as he watches me uncap the bottle and take a sip.

"What are your plans for the rest of the summer?" he asks as we begin to taxi to the runway.

"Mallory's talked me into using her husband's home in Italy for about a month."

He cocks a brow. "Who is Mallory married to?"

"Beau Boudreaux. His family owns Bayou Enterprises."

"Yes, I've heard of them. You'll love Italy."

"I've never been off of North America," I reply with a smile. "So it'll be fun to explore somewhere new. How about you? What are your plans?"

"I left a job in Chile to come here and take care of Aunt Claudia's things. I'll head back down there to finish the job."

"How much longer until that one's finished?" I ask.

"About two years," he replies and laughs when I cough, choking on the sip of water I just took.

"*Two years?*"

"Yes. We've discovered a new Mayan burial place, and we've found several mummies. I'm quite sure there's more to discover in the caves, but it's a process, and it takes a while to get permission from the government. Every time we want to explore a new cave we have to apply for a permit."

"Wow." *Two fucking years.* "And then what?"

"The next dig," he says with a shrug. "There's always something new to find."

I nod, feeling defeated. Now that I know our trip is almost over, I feel overwhelming melancholy. The trip to Italy was absolutely the right decision. I'll need the distraction from missing Mason all over again.

"Get comfortable, folks," the pilot says over the loud speaker, "we have a four and a half hour flight ahead of us."

I kick my shoes off, and reach for my carry on bag. I packed some yoga pants in case we had a long trip ahead of us today.

I stand and shimmy out of my jeans, then slide the yoga pants on and settle in my seat again.

"You're prepared," Mason says.

"Hell yes. Jeans are not comfortable to travel in."

He nods and pulls his iPad out of his bag, but before he can wake it up and do whatever it was he was going to do, I climb into his lap and lean my head on his shoulder.

"You okay?" he asks softly.

"Yeah. I'm just going to enjoy you while you're here."

He sighs and brushes his fingers up and down my arm.

"You can sit here for as long as you need."

I can't reply. I simply nod and settle in closer, listening to his heartbeat.

$\mathcal{S}$he fell asleep on me, and I didn't have the heart to wake her and move her. She doesn't weigh much, and she smells like fucking heaven.

My time with her is short. I didn't factor in the fact that I'd enjoy her so much during this trip. Getting to know her again has been intriguing and her body is every fucking fantasy I've ever had in my life.

We fit well together. I know how rare that is, but it doesn't change the fact that I'll be leaving for South America soon, and she'll go back to her life too.

"We'll be landing in about thirty minutes," the pilot says, waking Lena.

"I'm sorry," she says, looking around. She has a mark on her cheek from my shirt. "How long did I sleep?"

"A few hours." Her pretty blue eyes widen, making me smile.

She slides off of my lap and onto the seat beside me and rubs her hands over her face.

"I was knocked out," she says. "Dreaming and everything."

"I could tell."

"I'm sorry," she says again, but I take her hand in mine and kiss it.

"Don't apologize. I enjoy having you in my arms."

The wheels touch down, and the pilots come out of the cockpit.

"This is our last stop. We're in Montana. A car is here to pick you up and you'll be taken to where you'll be staying."

"Are there really no more clues?" Lena asks, disappointment heavy in her voice.

"No more clues," he replies. "Have a good visit."

Our bags are already being loaded into the car, which isn't a rental car, but one with a driver.

"Fancy," Lena says with a wink and slides over the black leather seat, giving me room to scoot in next to her.

"Good evening," the driver says with a nod. "We're in Missoula, and our destination is Philipsburg. It's only about an hour away."

Lena settles in next to me and leans her head on my arm. I love her touch. Her hands are small, but strong, and when she reaches for me it's not to barely brush her fingertips over my skin. She *touches* me, firmly. Purposefully.

God, I want her.

We're quiet on the drive, watching the mountains and green pastures until the car turns into a driveway with a bed and breakfast sign arched over the road.

"Here we are," the driver says and steps out to gather our bags.

A woman opens the front door with a smile and waves at us.

"Hello, there," she says. "I'm Sandra. You've had quite the day."

"It's been a long one," Lena agrees.

"Well, not to worry, dear. Your room is ready, and I've made dinner for you."

"You're my new best friend," Lena says.

"Would you mind if we took our dinner in our room?" I ask. "I think we'd like some quiet time this evening."

"I was going to suggest that," Sandra says with a wink. "Just follow me."

She leads us into a massive log house. The living room has a vaulted ceiling with floor to ceiling windows, showing off a beautiful view of the mountains.

"Your room is upstairs."

There's a king sized bed, and an adjoining bathroom with a soaking tub and steam shower.

"It looks so rustic from outside, but it's been nicely updated," Lena says with a smile. "Your home is beautiful."

"Thank you," Sandra says. "Why don't the two of you get comfortable and I'll bring your dinner up in about thirty minutes?"

"Perfect," I reply. "Thank you, Sandra."

She nods and closes the door behind her. Lena flings herself onto the bed and stares at the ceiling.

"We're in Montana."

"We're in the log cabin to prove it," I reply and pull my shirt out of my pants.

"Have you ever been here before?"

"No." I shake my head and stare out the window. The sun is just beginning to go down, casting the mountains in pink and purple. "And to the best of my knowledge, Aunt Claudia had never been here either."

"Interesting," Lena says. I turn to look at her, and my breath catches in my throat. She's even more beautiful than the sunset.

"You're stunning."

Her gaze whips over to mine and she blinks rapidly, which she does often when I say something unexpected.

"Are you surprised to hear that?"

"It's not something I hear every day," she says and goes back to staring at the ceiling.

"You should." I don't know why I'm suddenly frustrated, but I am. She *should* be told that she's stunning every goddamn day.

There's a knock on the door.

"I hope you like fried chicken," Sandra says with a

smile as she carries the tray into the room. "I brought up some waters and a bottle of wine as well. If you'd rather have something else, just call down."

"This looks delicious," Lena says with a smile.

"And heavy. Here, let me help."

"Oh, I'm fine." She sets the large tray on the table by the window and gestures to a wooden box also sitting on the table. "This is for you as well. Feel free to open it any time. It's yours to take."

"Thank you."

She nods happily and leaves. Lena uncovers the food.

"I vote for eating first," she says. "And then open the box."

"Sounds good." The meal is hearty and delicious. We devour the food quickly, hardly talking to each other in the process.

"I need to get her recipe before I go," Lena says with a happy sigh. "I'm so full, but I don't want to stop eating."

"Eat as much as you want."

She shakes her head and pushes her plate away. "No. I have to stop. I'll regret it if I don't."

I carry the tray across the room and set it on top of a dresser.

"Let's open the box."

Lena nods happily and I reach for the beautiful wooden box. The lid flips up, and inside is another box, made of velvet, and a letter.

"Read the letter aloud," Lena requests. "I like your voice."

"*Dearest Mason and Lena,*

"*By now you've traveled all over the country on a silly treasure hunt that I schemed up some months ago. I want to explain why I sent you to those particular places, and the story behind what's inside the velvet box.*

"*Mason, you asked me many times over the years to tell you what was in the chests in my bedroom, but I wasn't ready to talk about them. You see, it was a heartbreak too deep to talk about with a small boy. You wouldn't have understood.*

"*When I saw you with Lena six years ago, I knew that you belonged together. You are kindred spirits. You fit together. I know, I know, I'm just the meddling aunt. What do I know? Well, I know what I saw, and that was a light in your eyes when you looked at each other. It's special. Trust me, you don't find it very often.*

"*I only found it once. Charles was the greatest love of my life, and I cherish every moment we had together, even though it was cut entirely too short. In my early twenties, Charles and I took trips all over the country, very similar to the one you just went on. Of course, we didn't have a private jet; that's a perk that I'm happy I was able to throw in for you. Charles and I had the treasure hunting bug, and boy did we ever have some wonderful adventures! Hunting for precious stones was one of our favorite past times, but we also loved searching for dinosaur bones and other fascinating things. As a woman, it was frowned upon for me to go to college for archeology, but I didn't give a damn. I knew what I wanted, and I went for it. When Charles and I were asked to go on a dig in Mexico, we jumped at the opportunity! But then my mother fell ill, and I had the responsibility of staying home to take care of her in her last few years.*

"Charles went on ahead of me. It was supposed to be a six-month dig, but it turned into two years, then three. We sent letters back and forth, and oh how I missed him so. My heart ached with longing every day that we were separated.

"My mother passed away, and I was settling her estate, ready to join Charles in Mexico when I received word that he'd been killed in an accident on the job site. It felt as though my heart was ripped from my body, and I bled in grief every day for the rest of my life

"And now we circle back around to the two of you. As you'll see in the velvet box, there's a necklace."

I stop reading and open the velvet box, revealing a beautiful necklace made of yellow gold. There are stones; emerald, opal, quartz, jade, and many others in the necklace.

"That's gorgeous," Lena says in awe. She has tears flowing down her cheeks. "Keep reading. This is the best story I've ever heard."

Me too, love.

"All of the stones you see here are ones we found in the locations that you've been to in the past few days. They were our treasure, and Charles had this made for me as a memento from our travels.

"I'm sure you're wondering why you're in Montana now.

Well, there's a sapphire mine there that was Charles's and my favorite place to mine. The mountains there are the most beautiful I'd ever seen, and we went there often. The engagement ring that Charles proposed with was not a diamond ring.

"It was a Montana sapphire ring, and when you're ready for it, Mason, it's yours, just like the rest of my belongings.

"I would love for the two of you to go find your own sapphires. Enjoy Montana for a few days. It's unlike anywhere else in the world. I truly believe that it's a magical place. Lena, you'll appreciate that.

"And finally, the point I'm trying to make is this.

"It's important to make your way in the world. Traveling and discovering is a part of the human experience that can't be compared to anything else. But just as important are the relationships you forge in life, and nurturing those relationships.

"Digging for something or someone who's been dead for thousands of years is important work.

"But being with the living and breathing person who loves you is the most important work you'll ever do. The dead won't thank you, Mason. They don't care that you dug them up so you can learn about them.

"But your love? Well, learning and exploring, growing with each other, that is what life is all about. I wish that Charles and I had learned that lesson before we decided to endure the time apart. We had no idea that six months would turn into forever.

"I hope that this trip has taught you many new things about each other.

"With all of my love,
"Aunt Claudia"

"Wow," Lena says with a deep sigh. I let my eyes travel over the words again, picking up key words here and there. "Your aunt was an incredible woman."

"She was," I agree and set the letter back inside of the box. "The necklace is for you."

"No." Her eyes are wide as she shakes her head. "No, Mason, this was your aunt's, and especially after that story, it belongs with you."

"I think you've more than earned it, and Aunt Claudia would want you to have it. Trust me."

She looks uncertain. "Think it over. This isn't something you should just give away on a whim."

"I don't do *anything* on a whim, Lena. You know that." I set the box on top of her handbag and turn back to smile at her. "It's yours."

"I'll cherish it, always."

"I know."

CHAPTER 9

~LENA~

*H*e's dreaming again.

After the revelation of Claudia's letter, we had a quiet evening. Mason didn't talk much, and he seemed distracted. Distant. So I gave him his space and pretended to read a book.

I don't know what's going through his mind because he was so quiet, but I wanted to ask him about a million questions, starting with *what do you think?* Did she help him realize that he doesn't want to be like Charles? Does he think she was just a silly old woman?

But I didn't ask, and he didn't offer.

He hardly even touched me when we went to sleep. He turned away from me, so I snuggled up behind him, enjoying his warmth. He didn't sleep for a long time, but he didn't reach for me in the dark either.

I've already lost him.

He has been having bad dreams. He murmurs

things, and tosses and turns. He's on his back now, breathing hard and talking, but I don't understand the words.

"Hey," I say softly. "Mason, it's okay."

He scowls and his head thrashes back and forth.

"Mason." My voice is louder now. "It's okay. You're dreaming."

He wakes up and stares at me, then looks around the room as if he's not sure where he is.

"It's okay," I say again and cup his cheek. "You're just having a bad dream."

"Lena."

"I'm right here."

"God." He rolls toward me and wraps his arms around me, pinning me to the bed. He's hugging me tightly.

"Mason."

He lifts up far enough so I can catch my breath, and then he's kissing me. Urgently, incessantly, kissing me as if his life depends on it. He cups my breast and pinches my nipple roughly.

"I want you," he murmurs. "God help me, Lena, I want you."

"I'm right here." He reaches between us, down to my center, and rubs his fingertips over my sex, growling when he finds me already wet. "You're always ready for me."

"I can't get enough of you," I reply honestly.

He shakes his head and leans his forehead against

mine. "Do you have any idea what you do to me? You're a fucking drug, Lena. I can't say no to you. I can't fucking stay away from you."

"You don't have to."

He sinks inside me and we both sigh in relief and excitement.

"You feel amazing," he whispers and sets a rhythm, moving his hips quickly but not fast enough to make us both crazy.

I wrap my legs around his waist and he grabs my right knee, pushing it back farther, so I'm opened wide.

"So fucking beautiful," he growls. He moves faster, as if he's unable to stop himself, and I'm so damn thankful because I'm chasing the most explosive orgasm of my life.

I cry out as I come, squeezing him, my body shivering, and he follows me over, calling out my name as he explodes.

As we come back to Earth, he kisses me lightly and collapses next to me.

"I don't know what to do," he says sleepily.

"About what?"

But he's already sleeping again, as if the past few days have taken a bigger emotional and physical toll than I realized. He's softly snoring next to me. I brush my fingers through his hair and let my fingertips slip along the light stubble on his chin.

He's amazing. Physically, he really *could* be Captain America. But beneath that, he might be one of the best people I've ever met. He's been kind and accommodating to me. He truly would have understood if I had refused to join him on this trip.

I'm so relieved that I didn't refuse. I would have missed out on the adventure of a lifetime.

I would have missed out on being with Mason again, even for just a few short, wonderful days. And I wouldn't trade this for *anything*.

He said he doesn't know what to do, and I don't know what that means. Maybe he was just dreaming and it doesn't pertain to me or his aunt's letter at all.

Or maybe he doesn't know what to do about *me*.

And the fact that he even has to debate that issue within himself tells me everything I need to know. If he truly wanted me, and wanted to be *with* me, it wouldn't be a difficult decision to make.

I hold my breath as I slip from the bed, not wanting to wake him. I'm going to make this decision easy for him.

I quickly pull on some clothes, and gather my bags, then sneak out of the room and down to the front desk.

Of course Sandra is asleep, and we're in the middle of nowhere. There's a button on the desk that says to ring for service.

So I do.

Several minutes later, Sandra walks down the hall, tying the sash on her robe.

"Lena? Are you all right, dear?"

"I need to leave," I reply. "It's not your fault *at all*. I just need to leave right now."

"It's three in the morning."

"I know." I nod and swallow hard. "I'm sorry to do this to you. Is there a car service we can call to take me to the airport?"

"Not in Philipsburg," she replies, shaking her head. "Is there an emergency?"

"Yes," I lie, feeling guilty. "A family emergency."

"Okay. Don't you worry, we'll get you to the airport."

I nod, relieved as she picks up the phone to make a call. "Do you have a piece of paper that I could write a note on for Mason?"

"He's not leaving with you?"

I shake my head no, and she nods. "I see. Here you go."

"Thank you."

"AND HE HASN'T CALLED?" Mallory asks later that night. She's at my house, watching me unpack my bag.

"He called once, but I let it go to voice mail."

"Did you listen to it?"

"I deleted it." I shrug when Mallory's jaw drops. "What? I don't want to talk to him. The end result doesn't change. He has a job that takes him all over the world and my job is here."

"Maybe he was going to tell you that he loves you," she suggests.

"I don't think that's the case."

"Why not? You're loveable."

"He said it himself the day he told me why he left the first time. He's worked his *whole life* to be an archeologist, Mal. It's the only thing he's ever wanted to do, and he's damn good at it."

I shrug and grab a pile of clothes to throw in the washing machine. When I come back to the bedroom, Mallory is holding the velvet box with the necklace inside.

"This is some powerful stuff."

"I know."

"The love they shared is remarkable."

I nod, feeling tears threaten. "The story she told was beautiful, and so sad."

"You brought it with you."

I nod again. "I thought about leaving it, but he insisted that he wanted me to have it, and honestly, this is the only thing I have to remind me of the trip. I left all of the stones we found with him."

"It's sad that it ended this way," she says with a sigh.

"Why? Why is it sad?"

"Because Aunt Claudia wanted you two to fall in love again and get married and have a happy life."

"Can you feel that?" I ask.

"Oh yeah. There are so many emotions tied to this

necklace it's mind-boggling. But they're all good. You should wear it; it'll bring you peace."

She sets it aside.

"Well, it's not sad. She was an old woman who wanted her favorite nephew to fall in love, but I knew the score from the beginning, Mal. I knew that we would have a good time, and that we would have crazy amazing sex, and at the end of it, we'd go our separate ways."

"And you're okay," she says.

"I'm fine."

"You're lying."

I turn to her, ready to deny it, but stop myself. This is *Mallory*. I can't lie to her.

"I'm not okay," I admit and bite my lip. "But I will be. I got over him once, I can get over him again."

"I think that's a lie too," she says. "But I understand."

"I'd like to take you up on your offer of using Beau's place in Italy, if that's still okay."

"Perfectly okay," she says with a nod. "I think it's a good idea. You can clear your head, explore Italy."

"Write a book." I smile at the look of surprise on her face. "I've been thinking about writing a book for a long time, and I refuse to be one of those people who just says *I've always wanted to write a book* for the rest of my life. I'm going to write the damn book."

"Awesome," she says with a smile. "Is it a love story?"

"Probably."

"With lots of sex?"

"Maybe I'll find a hot Italian that I can do *research* with." We both laugh and Mallory stands up to hug me.

"I'm sorry you're sad."

"I'm sorry that you can feel that I'm sad. I'm going to be okay. Really."

"I know." She kisses my cheek. "I'll have Beau make sure the house in Italy is ready for you. When would you like to leave?"

"As soon as possible."

She nods. "I'm going to come visit. I've never been, and I'd love to see it."

"You'd better come visit."

"Are you going to be lonely?"

Being lonely isn't new to me.

But I shake my head. "Nope. I'm going to be great."

CHAPTER 10

~LENA~

I could live here.

I've been in Italy for three weeks, and if I wasn't so damn homesick for my Gram, I could absolutely move here.

The Boudreaux house is on the coast, not far from a bustling city that I can't pronounce. I've been pretty secluded, but have gone to town a few times a week for supplies, and just to see other people.

While at home, I've managed to write two hundred pages of a book. I have no idea if any of it makes sense, but it's been fun to use my imagination and invent make believe characters. The scenery has been a wonderful inspiration. I've spent many hours out on the deck, overlooking the sea, with my laptop in my lap, typing furiously long into the night.

Coming here was the right thing to do. My mind is

clear, and I know without a doubt that I did the right thing when I left Mason. And he must agree because aside from the first call on the day I left, he hasn't tried to reach me.

The breeze is blowing today, keeping me cool in the hot Italian sun. I have a wide-brimmed hat on my head, sweet tea beside me, and my laptop open with my document pulled up.

It might be the best day *ever.*

The ocean is a bit choppy because of the wind, but there are still plenty of sailboats to watch.

My doorbell rings, making me frown. I wasn't expecting Mallory until the end of the week, but maybe she decided to surprise me.

I jump up and run to the front door, excited, but stop in my tracks.

"Hi," Mason says with a tentative smile.

"You're here."

"I'm here."

I blink rapidly, looking him up and down. Jesus, he's a tall drink of water.

And he's here.

"Why are you here?"

"Because you're here." He smiles again, widely, and I narrow my eyes. "Can I come inside?"

"No."

He nods. "I'm sorry to hear that. Does it help if I mention that I've come a very long way to see you?"

"You wasted the trip," I reply and move to shut the door, but he shoves his hand out, stopping it.

"No. I didn't. Please let me talk with you. Ten minutes, fifteen tops."

I sigh and step back. "Ten minutes."

I turn and walk away, certain he'll follow me, returning to the deck. I sit in my lounge chair and motion for him to sit next to me, but instead he sits on the foot of my chair. He's watching me closely.

"You look beautiful."

"Thank you."

"You're tan."

"Did you come all this way to discuss my tan?"

He laughs, surprising me. "That's right, you're sassy."

"Every day."

"I didn't come here to talk about your tan. I came here to find out why the woman I'm in love with left my bed in the middle of the night and disappeared."

"I have no idea. Did you put out a missing persons bulletin?"

"Now you're being difficult," he says and rubs his hand over his mouth.

"I'm really bad at this," I admit with a sigh. "Look, I thought I was doing us both a favor, Mason. Your aunt's letter was beautiful, but it didn't change anything. You're still you and I'm still me, and we both knew that at the end of the trip we'd be going back to our own lives.

"So, I left before it could get awkward and weird."

"I see." He stands now and leans on the railing of the deck, looking out at the water. Finally, he turns to look at me. "I'm sorry that I was so quiet that night. After I had a chance to think about it, it occurred to me that you probably thought I was an ass."

"No, you had a lot on your mind."

"I did. And you should know that when I need to think, I do get quiet. It doesn't mean that I'm angry, or avoiding you, or that it's even *about* you. I've just climbed inside my own head."

"Okay. That's actually good to know."

"And you should also know that you couldn't have been more wrong. When I woke up the next day to find you gone, I was a crazy man. Poor Sandra." He shakes his head and shoves his fingers through his hair. "Let's just say that I wasn't a very nice guy that morning."

"You shouldn't have taken it out on Sandra. It was *my* decision."

"I know. I was angry."

"Now you know how it feels," I reply. "At least I left you a letter."

"Is this what it was? Revenge?"

I sigh in frustration and stand to pace the deck. "No. That's not what I was thinking when I left. I was honest when I said that I was just avoiding the awkward goodbyes later."

"But I didn't want to say goodbye," he says, surprising me. "That was never my intention."

"You're going back to Chile, Mason. And then somewhere else after that. Egypt? China? Freaking Peru? I don't know, but you'll be *gone.*"

"No." He hurries to me and takes my hands in his. "Damn it, we could have avoided all of this if you had just *stayed.* Aunt Claudia's letter hit me like a punch across the face. I read the letters that Charles sent her before he died, right before we left on our trip, and it made me start thinking. Her letter only reinforced what I had already been thinking."

"And what is that?"

"That I want to be with *you.* I want to spend every damn day of my life with you, Lena. I love you so much I can't see straight, and I know now that I never *stopped* loving you. I told you that you knocked everything out of focus for me before, and it wasn't until I was finally with you again that everything came back into focus.

"You make me laugh. You make me think. You make me fucking crazy. I can't keep my hands off of you. There are a million reasons that I love you, and I plan to spend the rest of my life listing all of them for you."

"Wow." He cups my face in his hands, and wipes away a tear that I didn't even realize was on my cheek. "I spent a really long time trying to get over you, Mason, and I never could. I thought that I knew the score this time, and that when it was over I could go back to my life."

"But?"

"But I can't," I whisper. He leans his forehead against mine. "I love you, too."

He wraps his arms around me, lifting me off the ground and twirling me in a circle, and then kisses me in that sweet way he does that makes my toes curl.

"Wait." I press my hand to his chest. "We love each other, but it doesn't change your job."

"Last year, I was offered a job at Tulane, teaching archeology in the graduate program." He smiles and brushes my hair off my cheek. "I called and they said the job is still mine if I want it."

"Do you want it?" I whisper.

"You're looking at the newest professor at Tulane. I want to be wherever *you* are, Lena. There may be times that I'll want us to go on an adventure, but I'm done being gone for months or sometimes years. Aunt Claudia was right, the most important thing is being with the person you love."

He reaches in his pocket and pulls out the most beautiful sapphire and diamond ring I've ever seen.

"Is that—?"

"Aunt Claudia's? Yes." He's staring into my eyes as he takes my hand. "Lena, I love you. I can't wait to start our adventure together. Will you marry me?"

I don't even hesitate. "Yes. Yes, I'll marry you."

He slips the ring on my finger and kisses me.

"Can we change our names to Jones?"

"Just call me Indie."

. . .

I HOPE you enjoyed Easy Fortune! Don't forget to check out the rest of the Boudreaux series! You can find them all here:

https://www.kristenprobyauthor.com/boudreaux

NEWSLETTER SIGN UP

I hope you enjoyed reading this story as much as I enjoyed writing it! For upcoming book news, be sure to join my newsletter! I promise I will only send you news-filled mail, and none of the spam. You can sign up here:

https://mailchi.mp/kristenproby.com/ newsletter-sign-up

Other Books by Kristen Proby

The With Me In Seattle Series

Come Away With Me
Under The Mistletoe With Me
Fight With Me
Play With Me
Rock With Me
Safe With Me
Tied With Me
Breathe With Me
Forever With Me
Stay With Me
Indulge With Me
Love With Me
Dance With Me

Dream With Me
You Belong With Me
Imagine With Me
Shine With Me
Escape With Me

Check out the full series here: https://www.
kristenprobyauthor.com/with-me-in-seattle

The Big Sky Universe

Love Under the Big Sky
Loving Cara
Seducing Lauren
Falling for Jillian
Saving Grace

The Big Sky
Charming Hannah
Kissing Jenna
Waiting for Willa
Soaring With Fallon

Big Sky Royal
Enchanting Sebastian
Enticing Liam
Taunting Callum

Heroes of Big Sky

Honor

Courage

Check out the full Big Sky universe here: https://
www.kristenprobyauthor.com/under-the-big-sky

Bayou Magic

Shadows

Spells

Check out the full series here: https://www.
kristenprobyauthor.com/bayou-magic

The Romancing Manhattan Series

All the Way

All it Takes

After All

Check out the full series here: https://www.
kristenprobyauthor.com/romancing-manhattan

The Boudreaux Series

Easy Love

Easy Charm

Easy Melody

Easy Kisses

Easy Magic

Easy Fortune

Easy Nights

Check out the full series here: https://www.
kristenprobyauthor.com/boudreaux

The Fusion Series

Listen to Me

Close to You

Blush for Me

The Beauty of Us

Savor You

Check out the full series here: https://www.
kristenprobyauthor.com/fusion

From 1001 Dark Nights

Easy With You

Easy For Keeps

No Reservations

Tempting Brooke

Wonder With Me

Shine With Me

Kristen Proby's Crossover Collection

Soaring with Fallon, A Big Sky Novel

Wicked Force: A Wicked Horse Vegas/Big Sky Novella
By Sawyer Bennett

All Stars Fall: A Seaside Pictures/Big Sky Novella
By Rachel Van Dyken

Hold On: A Play On/Big Sky Novella
By Samantha Young

Worth Fighting For: A Warrior Fight Club/Big Sky
Novella
By Laura Kaye

Crazy Imperfect Love: A Dirty Dicks/Big Sky Novella
By K.L. Grayson

Nothing Without You: A Forever Yours/Big Sky
Novella
By Monica Murphy

Check out the entire Crossover Collection here:
https://www.kristenprobyauthor.com/kristen-proby-
crossover-collection

ABOUT THE AUTHOR

Kristen Proby has published close to sixty titles, many of which have hit the USA Today, New York Times and Wall Street Journal Bestsellers lists. She continues to self publish, best known for her With Me In Seattle, Big Sky and Boudreaux series.

Kristen and her husband, John, make their home in her hometown of Whitefish, Montana with their two cats and French Bulldog named Rosie.

facebook.com/booksbykristenproby
instagram.com/kristenproby
bookbub.com/profile/kristen-proby
goodreads.com/kristenproby

Made in the USA
Monee, IL
06 March 2021